There's
No Rush

More tales of a daring hypochondriac

Marion Pollack

IMPORTANT NOTICES

Copyright 2024 © *There's No Rush* by Marion Pollack

ISBN 979-8-9863603-9-3

Editor Rodney Richards

Publisher ABLiA Media LLC, Hamilton NJ USA

First edition

Disclaimer

Photos shown are personal shots, public domain, used with permission, or commercially licensed by the author. No AI was used on or to compose text in this book. Text solely attributable to the author.

To my progeny

I dedicate this book to those who come after me. This, so they won't have to clean up the detritus left behind. Who wants to plow through papers, rewrites, and scribblings of a lifetime?

On these pages I have consolidated some of my favorite meanderings which I think you will enjoy. I hope you always find your own pleasure in reading and writing.

To my children Jonathan and Susan, and grandchildren, Ariel, Jakob, Joey, Nathan, Jonah, and Gabriel. I love you!

Marion

Contents

Introduction

Woody Allen was asked to write a few words about his hypochondria. He balked.

"I am not a hypochondriac, but a totally different genus of crackpot. I am an alarmist."

Here is the difference. He wrote, "I don't experience imaginary maladies. My maladies are real."

What distinguishes his hysteria is that at the appearance of a mild symptom, he concludes he is dying. This leads to many visits to the emergency room. When I saw this piece in the New York Times, I perked up.

That's Me!

But wait. I am not only an alarmist. I am a hypochondriac too. When my friends complain, describing their ailments, I empathize. I feel their pain. I feel their dizziness, their nausea, their weakness, their palpitations, and their lumps. I usually say, *I have that too.*

Nowadays, especially since COVID, we alarmists and hypochondriacs get less attention. When we call our primary care physicians with a respiratory complaint, we're told, "Go to Urgent Care." If we go to Urgent Care with heart palpitations, they say, "Go to the ER." Once there, quite often, we're told to go home. "My dear, there is really nothing wrong with you."

So now we are out here fending for ourselves. It's not such a bad thing really.

The last time I checked, Woody Allen is still alive. I am too.

It is with great pleasure that I write stories and poems pointing out the craziness and foibles of people in my world. I loved putting together this new book. I am grateful always to my husband Bob who puts up with me.

It is my hope that my children, relatives, and friends will read the book with tolerance and enjoy it for what it is.

Marion's Mom Paula, and Bob's mom, Florence

Arrogance of Seagulls

Inspired by the cover photo

A Seagull with Vladimir Putin eyes
slightly crossed, struts by
looking for prey
Proud head bobs from side to side
eying our blanket
Steely, stealthy, diligent, he takes his time

With pointy laser beak he steps boldly
over the line
attacks the chips
Everyone curses and screams
at his arrogance and power
But he is gone
The rich march onto the beach
with the finest straws and dresses

Caviar fed kids clamor behind
kicking sand on us without concern
"Here's a good spot!"
"I don't like it!"
"Where's your good spot then?"
"Right here!"
Am I invisible?

Plop, plop go the Birkenstocks
To hold the blanket down
Plop, plop drops the cooler
Twist twist grinds the umbrella into the sand
Spray spray goes the sunscreen
polluting the purest breezes

"Alex, stand still so I can spray you!"
"No, I want Mommy to do it."
"Mommy is resting"
"I don't care, I want Mommy!"

Scream scream, stamp stamp
Sand flies in my eyes
"Little boy please be still" I say
Mother awakens like a sleeping bear
"How dare you yell at my child"

I am silent.

Wealthy grandpa lumbers over
to join the party, very tan, very wrinkled
bringing a basket of toys
"Yay, yay, grandpa is here!"
The fat, hairy belly jiggles
above his shorts

Who knows what lurks beneath

On Childhood

Good Humor

When I was a little girl   I had allergies bad
Itchy eczema made me scratch
Swollen throat made me gag
I just wanted to have fun

When I was a little girl   I played with friends
In my apartment building   I loved my friends
2E gave me a sesame candy   I choked
Took the stairs two at a time to 4B
mommy, mommy, I can't breathe

When I was a little girl   I played with friends
In my apartment building   I loved my friends
5B was a "touch nothing house"   that mother screamed and hit
We stuck pencils in the eyes of porcelain dolls to find a brain
peeked under dresses too

When I was a little girl   I had motion sickness
I threw up in my best friend's car   He never spoke to me again

3B played Fleur de lis on piano every night at 6 pm
On the playground, we loved to watch him stretch his skin
beyond anything human
When he fell and bled we took him home. His skin was hanging
His mother yelled, hit him. She slammed the door in our faces
We didn't hear Fleur de lis for awhile

When I was a little girl, I had bandages on my eczema
in the creases of my elbows and knees. Girls had to wear
dresses then
The kids kept saying *what's wrong with you?*
I just wanted to have fun

My fifth birthday party was the best and the worst

Dad made a round, colorful, cardboard mic on a broom stick.
We played every game like pin the tail on the donkey
But I couldn't eat the ice cream, Mom made me eat gelatinous
goat milk junket instead
Cousin Phlly noticed, *That's disgusting, how can you eat that?*

He made me cry
I just wanted to have fun

One day, not too much later we hear the Jingle bells
of the Good Humor man. Mom says, *Want to give ice cream a
try? Yes!!*

We run over to greet him. He is wearing his clean white
uniform and smiles broadly at me
What will it be today, little girl?
The vanilla dixie cup comes with a little wooden paddle.
I slowly peel open the lid and instantly smell the vanilla. I see
the vanilla bean dots. I dip the flat spoon in and take my first
delicious taste.
I feel cool, sweet creamy pleasure on my tongue…

I am having fun!

Daddy

When I was a little girl I loved my daddy
I waited for him to come home at 6:00
He'd lift me high in the air
for a hug around the neck

I squeezed very tight; I knew he liked
that hug around the neck
Starched white collar, still crisp dark suit
silk tie, vague after shave lotion aroma

My daddy was perfect   I walked
him back to the bedroom
Carefully he'd hang the suit jacket in the closet, loosen
his tie and roll up his sleeves for dinner

How's business? I'd say, I knew he liked
that conversation
The big girl talk made him laugh
How's your business? he would say

One time   I prepared for him with red
nail polish on every finger
He came at 5:45 that day   Still not dry
I rubbed all my nails on both sides of my dress

He looked right at me with a frown
Are you bleeding? he said
There are red stains on your dress

He didn't lift me up that day

Mayonaise

Mom, what's mayonnaise? All my friends have it on their tuna fish sandwiches.

Oh, Marion, I'm sorry, but you can't have mayonnaise because you're allergic to eggs.

And mom, what's ketchup? All my friends have it on their hamburgers.

Oh, Marion, I'm sorry, but you can't have ketchup, you're allergic to tomatoes.

It's not fair! I can't eat anything. I can't even have tuna fish!

No Marion, you're allergic to fish. You're only seven years old, When you're ten we're hoping you will be able to eat everything. Right now, you know you don't want to get hives, start to cough and sneeze or even have trouble breathing. Do you?

No mommy.

So it went for many years. I could eat meat and vegetables, soy or goats milk, yucky junket and rice products. Forget about gluten. No chocolate, no nuts, no ice cream. Allowed maple sugar treats and lots of fruit. A deprived child.

One day when twelve, in my seventh-grade home economics cooking class, Mrs. Breadpudding announced we'd be making an easy lunch treat, tuna fish sandwiches with tomato on whole wheat toast. We'd have chocolate pudding and chocolate chip cookies for dessert. I was nervous but thrilled with anticipation.

First, we mashed up tuna fish in big bowls. We added huge globs of mayonnaise. We chopped in some celery and bits of onion and mixed it all together.

We giggled as we stirred up the mushy concoction. The aroma was so tantalizing I had to have a taste. With a small spoon, when no one was looking, I scooped up one little bit of the delicious, prohibited mixture. Oh God, it was so delectably creamy, tangy and crunchy at the same time.

I waited, fearing the worst. Nothing yet.

We sliced tomatoes, toasted bread, added extra mayonnaise to each slice. Pressed it together and carefully slit the sandwiches into triangles.

Remember girls, you have to wait until the lunch bell rings before you can eat your special lunch.

Now we'll make the chocolate pudding. Follow the recipe. Don't forget to slowly stir the bits of chocolate into the milk and cornstarch, add the cocoa and sugar and keep stirring until it boils. Immediately remove from the heat and pour into dessert dishes. It's not easy, but I know you can do it.

If yours comes out right, I will add a big scoop of whipped cream on top.

Oh God, am I going to die of pleasure? Or anaphylactic shock.

We worked in groups of three on small portable ranges. We had pots, wooden spoons and all the ingredients. It was the most fun I ever had. Some of the pudding boiled over. There were some drips and burns, but it actually all worked. We now each had a beautiful bowl of chocolate pudding, with a lovely skin on top. Mrs. Breadpudding plopped real whipped cream on the top of each of ours and gave us chocolate chip cookies for good measure. We were given brown paper bags to carry it all to lunch.

In those days, you could eat in the lunchroom or walk home. I chose the latter; you can guess why.

Mom, guess what we made in cooking class today. Tuna fish sandwiches, chocolate pudding with whipped cream and chocolate chip cookies. I'll even share it with you.

I don't know Marion. We tried ice cream when the Good Humor man came and that was okay. But I don't know about eating all of this at once.

Oh mom, I've got to try sometime, right?

We set the table and placed everything out in front of us. The chocolate pudding had spilled out a little into the bag, but we spooned it into two small glass bowls. Mom brought out two glasses of apple juice and placed two Benadryl tablets in the middle of the table.

So, it began. We each had a crunchy, gooey half of a tuna and tomato sandwich, oozing with mayonnaise. The chocolate pudding was the best thing I ever tasted. Then we shared the chocolate chip cookie. We washed it down with apple juice.

Nothing happened.

I swallowed a Benadryl tablet to be on the safe side.

The Persistence of Steady Enders

When I was a little girl we wore little girl dresses
all the time to climb monkey bars, to ride bicycles
to jump rope

Little boys loved to pull up our little girl dresses to take a look

I see London I see France
I see Marion's underpants

When I was a little girl I jumped rope all the time
in my little girl dresses
My heart beat hard waiting my turn in a neat long line

In, jump, jump, out
In, one-two, out on time

competing to win

All you need are two steady enders and a rope
a clothesline will do
Two persistent and consistent kids who can endure

In, skip skip, out
In, one-two, out on time

If you trip in your little girl dress you are kaput, out!

Finally, there were two of us left   sweating with delight
In, jump, jump out
In, one-two, out

I never make it to number one
But I'm grateful for
the persistence of steady enders

The Butcher Shop

Mommy why doesn't the butcher have a thumb?
  Shush Marion, he can hear you!
It's okay kid, I'll tell you all about it!

I am five years old and barely able to see over the
huge butcher's block. I watch with horror and delight,
as Dave, the butcher, uses his cleaver to splinter bones
and trim fat. His variety of knives and saws pound,
chop and slice hunks of meat.

See dis ax? Dis is the very one that chopped off de
finger, twenty years ago. I didn't mean it, but I was
careless. Little girl, you better keep your hands down
or it might chop off your thumb too. Don't look so
scared girlie, just sayin'.

The store is longer than it is wide. The butcher block
is in front just as you step into the shop. The saw dust
covered interior is clean and cool. The freezer behind
the counter is constantly opening, sending out blasts of
cold air. There is a consistent, distinct metallic, blood
smell of fresh, raw meat. The long display counter
runs along the shop almost to the end.

I roam to the back while mom is negotiating a leg of
lamb. There at the end sits the Chicken Flicker.

A woman of uncertain age, although ancient to me,
sits hunched on a stool amidst a pile of chicken
feathers. A half-naked, limp chicken lays over her lap,
its head dangling. One hand gently but firmly holds
down the dead creature, while the other furiously
picks off the feathers. She plucks with such dizzying
and deliberate speed that I can barely see her red,
gnarled hand. I am transfixed. She performs her job
with gusto and love.

9

I find out later that her name is Mildred and that she can flick fifteen to twenty-five chickens in a day.

She is dressed in black with a long, white, blood speckled apron in front. She wears a white bandana, allowing some feathery, salt and pepper wisps of hair to peek out. I'm terrified and fascinated.

She looks up, her broad smile displays tiny teeth. Her neck is a pink wattle, suggesting her age. She gazes right at me over a pointy, beak-like nose. She has pretty blue eyes that seem to meet in the middle of her face.

Want to try it little girl?
Oh no, I don't know how to do that. You're so good at it.
You can do anything if you practice.

Marion, where are you? It's time to go honey!
It's mom calling me.

Okay, mom, I'm coming.

Mildred waves her free hand. *Come again soon! It was fun meeting you.*

Okay! Bye.

My mother carries two large lumpy sacks. I know one has the leg of lamb.

Marion, guess what? I also bought a lovely chicken for us to roast for dinner tonight.

I'm not so sure how I feel about this!

Little Girl in Red

At the Border

Little girl in Red
Red shirt, red pants, red sneakers
Crying for her mommy

Who are you?
Why are you lost?
Where is your mommy? Mine is lost too

Mommy will come back
Says the social worker
Here's a cookie

Little girl in Red
Crying for her mommy
No, No, No, she cries
I want my mommy

Here is a nice bed in this cage
Like a puppy
Foil wrap keeps you warm
You will have friends here

No, No, No
I want my mommy!

But look at all the children
you can play with
Here is a bologna sandwich
Don't cry

No, No, No!
Go away!
I want my mommy!

Huaraches

When I was a little girl, I wanted to wear Huaraches
You know, the soft tobacco colored woven leather sandals?
But they're sandals, Momma said
You cannot wear sandals

Why? I begged
She made me wear brown oxfords
You know the brown oxfords with arch supports?
Those sandals are not good for your feet

One sunny day we went to Indian Walk Shoes
I got to see my feet in the x-ray machine
You know how you see all the bones in your toes?
Now can I have Huaraches momma?

The shoe salesman said we can fit them with arches
You know in those days we thought x-rays were good,
remember?

Momma said *let's give it a try*
I always loved my tobacco-colored woven leather sandals
called Huaraches

On Love

Glamour Shot

One day in DC, cherry blossoms in full bloom
you take my picture in black and white

Perfect, fragrant blossoms blushing pink and rosy
you take my picture with your Argus 35 millimeter
In black and white

No one will see my face blush red hot as it is wont to do
There it is, the glamour shot, peeking through tilted branches
In black and white

Married just six months, I am flush with the freedom we have
found on Connecticut Ave in DC, and just about to sneeze
In black and white

So many years later, I study the black-and-white photo you took
with the Argus 35 millimeter

Pink and rose blossoms a vague memory, the scent
a fuzzy dream
The photo on tough paper in black and white is still sharp

A glamour photo you took
In black and white

Tango

Slow, slow, quick quick, slow
Tango the dance of love and life
never to be rushed
Life is short

Arching bodies, pressed tight, step and sway in perfect rhythm
Then lurch, pause, repeat
searching for lost time
Life is short

Slow, slow, quick quick, slow
The languid pace of childhood summers
jerked to awareness by the start of school
Life is short

Sunny days no end in sight
Lovely, listless days waiting for a child to emerge
a sudden shocking delivery
The Tango of life
Slow, slow, quick quick, slow

Intimate Latin beat, holding so close
afraid to let go, afraid to die
Persistence of memory is
Slow, slow, quick quick, slow

The Cup

There's a natural arc from the cup to the sink
Placement there within a single eye wink
But no

It remains with passive aggression on the perimeter
on the very edge of the sink
But why?

Through the years we've compromised
yet still play to win
Is this your hold out for masculine pride?

Who knows?

There's many a slip between the lip and the cup
And I for one, am not perfect
But after you drink your brew, put the damn cup in the sink!

Okay, you say

Though my cup runneth over with love for you
I'm brought too close to the edge
Please respect what I do
Put the damn cup in the sink
Huh?

A toast with a chalice of wine
to us and persistence of time
My heart is full to the brink
Now please put the cup in the sink!
What?

I tiptoe up, grab the cup, temper in check
Throw it hard into the sink
It shatters

On Cuddling

On Marriage *

Let there be spaces in your togetherness
Let the winds of heaven dance between you
Stand together yet not too near together

I love to cuddle in bed with you, like spoons stacked in a drawer
I feel the warmth of your leg over mine, hot breath in my ear

I sweat profusely

I love to cuddle in bed with you, like spoons stacked in a drawer

Dear, your knee replacements are pressing on my derriere

I love to cuddle in bed with you, like spoons stacked in a drawer
Your weighty arm is an expression of love

Your arm over mine stops the blood flow

I love to cuddle in bed with you. There is no other

When your toenails burrow my ankle
I have to break free

Be together but let each one be alone

On Love and Marriage, The Prophet, Kahlil Gibran

Little Brown-eyed Girl

Pretty brown-eyed girl
Sweet skin soft and creamy
Your fragrance lingers

Everyone loves you
Neighborhood kids come to play
And hang out with you

No one loves you more
Then mommy and daddy do
Even your brother

The Tree Climber

My little boy loves to climb trees
to the very top
where the branches sway

My protests go unheeded as he laughs
laughs, laughs at me
Get down right now!

Out on a quivering limb, he laughs
and waves
You're gonna crack your head open!
I'm secretly so proud

At this moment I look away
My little boy who loves to climb trees

The Dance

A lonely red sycamore leaf sways and twirls
in descent
An updraft lifts it to dance and pirouette
one last time

The aggressive burnt-orange maple spins and twists
its wings fighting to stay afloat
Dancing in waltz time
it dives to the ground

A timid yellow oak sashays from side-to-side, whispering
Save me
Others pass it by in no hurry
Shyly it lands on the pile

Have you noticed the golden beauty?
the one who won't let go
Excited and jittery
clinging to life

Every leaf at its own pace and time
like human life
No two the same
dizzily twirling on ballet point

I swirl, twist and struggle
to stay afloat
Love comes to raise me up
but some day I will fall

To earth

On Women

Art by Glenn Miller

A Woman Must, 1934

Daughter, you are not married
You are thirty-four and not married

Mother, I have a life, I love this life
Why mother, do you harp?
Why must you cry?

I cry for you daughter because you must
A woman must marry to be safe
I cannot stop crying

You cry too much always to me
Because I am the oldest
Is that why?
You cry about your own marriage
Cry, Cry, Cry

But daughter, your brother Abie
He is married
Your baby sister Fae
She is married
I cried at their weddings for you
Cry, Cry, Cry

Momma, I am at Hunter College
I have a good job
I have many friends
I fight for women's rights
I am happy, momma

My daughter, I love you so much
Fix your hair
Throw out the glasses
Wear tighter clothes to show your figure

Momma I have a lover
A beautiful man who is my lover
We are perfect for each other
In every way

Daughter, will he marry you?

Momma, I don't know

Paula and Leo

Diana*

Tall as Cedar, willowy branches spread wide
Your sinewy back and limbs motion us forward
In rhythmic patterns
we dance with our graceful goddess

Your beautiful face rarely seen, we follow from behind
thumping with the beat, pirouetting on cue
Spent, you turn to face us, spraying sweat and tears
and rush out in a trail of Cedar fragrance

With every twist and turn, we stretch our limbs toward you,
lost in ecstasy
Limpid hazel eyes so sad, your face sweaty and tear streaked
you rush off in your trail of Cedar fragrance

One day you stand proud before us, tall as Cedar
Clearly, we hear your words, *My father has died, I have to go.*
I'll be back soon.
You rush away in your trail of Cedar Fragrance

You do not come back.

**The dance class referred to was held at a local gym every
Saturday morning, 9:30 am, for 30 years. In mythology, Diana
was Goddess of the forest.*

The Farm Stand

Six ears of corn, a ripe tomato, five little eggplants.
Everything looks so good today.
But today's the last day

She shakes her head, her black curls jiggle
Why?

Well, winter is coming and we're running out of corn
Everything is on sale. Take your pick.

Oh, I'll miss you.

A petite dark-haired lady who loves to talk
My son just had another baby, I'm so happy, something
for me to do, come winter
Today's the last day

Well then, I'll take a bottle of the Sweet Vidalia dressing, a
cantaloupe, and these Honey Crisp apples.

It was too hot here this summer. I drank a lot of water and then I
had to go. We have a porta-potty out back. (we laugh)
But now winter is coming I can help with the babies
Today is the last day.

Well then, a jar of honey, a small watermelon
and a butternut squash. I have my bags here.

That will be $28.49. I can help you load the car.

Thanks for everything. I will miss you
See you in the spring

Yes, see you in spring

Velma, Checkout Lady

How long have you worked here?
  A long time, A long time
I always choose your line, I like your line
I've known you a long time, a long time

  I'm here thirty-one years, thirty-one years
  I remember you too

I always choose your line
You are quick and friendly, quick and friendly
I always choose your line

  I like the food you buy
  Healthy things like yogurt, fruit, and broccoli

*I remember when she was young. The face puffy now, large
brown eyes baggy, the stomach fat. She was pretty once.*

I always choose your line
You are quick and friendly, quick and friendly
I always choose your line
  I remember your kids; they were funny and cute
They are all grown up now
  I never had kids, she says

So many years ago, will you retire soon?
  The pension's not so good for part time. I have to stay
  I like it here. This store is my family

I'll see you next time then, thanks for bagging
  Thank you for bagging too

Thank you for everything
Bye now
  Good bye

Aunt Dora and the Four Sam's

Story by By Paula Sternberg

Aunt Dora, far left

Nobody ever said "No" to Aunt Dora.

Dora was one of four sisters. She came to the United States alone at the age of fourteen. She immediately got a job at a shirt waist factory and went to night school to learn English. My mother, Sarah, was Dora's half-sister.

At eighteen, she met Sam No.1, Sam Milch, and was married at twenty. They left New York for Newark, NJ, where they opened a grocery and meat market. Sam's asthma kept him from doing most of the heavy work which was left to Dora. They had two sons and a daughter.

Sam died at age forty, leaving Dora a sum of money. Aunt Dora became the "Merry Widow." For a time, she ran the business herself. She was a strong woman with a family to support.

Dora was not single for long. An attractive woman, she met a handsome playboy who fascinated her. He talked her into marriage, becoming Sam No.2. He did little work at the store, however. He gambled and went out with other women. Upon finding this out, a good lawyer and $10,000 sent him on his way.

It wasn't long before Aunt Dora sold the business, purchased a car, a house in Florida, and an apartment in Brighton Beach. She invested her money in real estate and became a lady of leisure.

Again, she didn't stay single long. She married Sam No.3, Sam Lert. She lived with him for sixteen years. He died prematurely, so she was again on her own. By now, her children were grown.

At age seventy, she met her fourth and last husband, who, strangely enough, was named Sam. Sam Feit. Sam No.4. He was ten years younger than she and very much in love with her.

Dora was strong willed and determined, truly ahead of her time. Her beauty, confidence, and ambition took her far. She lived to the ripe old age of eighty-eight, dying quietly in her home in Florida.

Unicorn and the Zebra

Grandma you are a Unicorn
You have magical powers
Can you heal my wounded heart?

Ariel, no, I am a Zebra
I am black and white
I follow the herd

But grandma you are wise
Independent
Mysterious too
I want to be like you

Ariel, no, I am a Zebra
I need community
You have beauty and strength
You are a Unicorn

Grandma, Zebras are wild
and free
Not just black and white
No fears, they are
Strong

Ariel, there is the paradox
I can only sleep surrounded by the herd
You are free to roam
You will heal your heart

Grandma, is the world black or white?
Is it happy or sad? Strong or weak?
A gray whirling mass?
Something in between?

Ariel, yes, there is a middle ground
Take the risk
Find your own path
You are a Unicorn

Ariel

On Aging

Art by Glenn Miller

Walking

I walk from where I have been
I walk to where I am going
I walk away from the past
I walk into the future
My pace erratic

You have Haglund's Deformity
The doctor says
What is that? I say
It's that bump on your heel
Will I be able to walk?
Stretch and Ice, Stretch and Ice

Life, a long walk
Life, a conversation
Every step faces both ways
An ending
A beginning

You have Achilles Tendinitis
The doctor says
What is that? I say
It's the tightness in your heel
It really hurts
Stretch and Ice, Stretch and Ice

The pathways I walk are pathways I live
The trail leads to new destinations
walking and talking along the way
to those I love
To those who are indifferent

It will get better the doctor says
When will it get better? I say
It takes a long time
I don't have a long time!

Ripples

Like ripples in the sea they drift away
Caught in foam lipped eddies
they swirl to a distant shore
out of reach and out of time

A single twisted wave tosses them back
Fighting for breath a rip tide pulls them under
away from me
Leaving just a bubbly foam

A collaboration with Roseanne Bozzone

There's No Rush

We love your house,
the structure and taste
Pristine upkeep
Not much waste

How can it be
60 years have passed?
The furniture like new
Held up to the last

But there's no rush!

We love central Jersey
The weather and trails
We'd like to settle here
Where nothing fails

Oh the memories!

You just had it painted
Air conditioner is new
There's a brand new deck
A house with a view

Take your time!

We don't want your money
It can't buy us love
It's the house we covet
A value above

All else.

But there's no rush!

Fatty Liver Blues

Give up egg rolls
Cut out bacon
Drop pizza
And Charcuterie
Eat broccoli,
Kale, cabbage and corn
Drink only green tea

You've got the Fatty Liver Blues

Wine is taboo, cheese kaput
Nothing the color of white
Always think green
Stay on the path, be a good girl
Don't try to fight
Have a cup of green tea

You've got the Fatty Liver Blues

Give up cookies
Cut out cake
Drop all the candy
Don't ever eat steak
Stick with the veggies, stay with the fruit
Don't stray from the path
Drink your green tea

You will feel so much better.
Really?

You've got the Fatty Liver Blues

Cataract

*A cataract creates a cloud on the normally transparent lens,
blurring vision, eventually leading to blindness*

The air conditioner doesn't seem to be working. I begin to feel
heat in my armpits. I shift to cross my legs in the plastic chair
and breathe. Now I understand the glazed looks on the faces
around me, we have the same expression of terror. We wait for
eye surgery after all.

Marion?

Yes! Taken by surprise and scream my yes. Feel the roar of
my pounding pulse.

Hi Sweetie, just follow me. I'm Mary. We enter a dimly lit
space, a row of beds reminiscent of an emergency room.

She points to a bathroom.

Honey, do you have to use the restroom?

No, I just went twice.

Well, go a third time.

Mary is one of the several nurses at the surgery center.
She will prepare me for cataract surgery. This time it's the left
eye. My second go around. She is a large, squarely built
woman, with a full face and gray, short curly hair. A perm?
Severe, small, round, rimless glasses ride on her nose. She has a
loud, commanding boisterous voice. Did she once work in an
Austrian orphanage?

Okay darlin', lie down on the bed. I'll get you a blanket.

I feel dizzy and nauseous, so I need a prop for my head.

Anything you want my love. Is she sincere? She continually uses
endearing phrases. Beds fill up on either side of me. This is an
assembly line.

*Sweetie, soon I'll put lots of drops in your eyes to dilate the
pupils. My pet, I hear last time you had a rough time because
the cataract was stuck to the pupil.*

Must you remind me?

First, I'm going to set up your IV, honey.

Are you good at it?

Mary's face darkens, her mouth a scowl.
Baby, no one ever asks me that.

She tightens the rubber tube around my arm. She taps for a vein. I am hemophobic. I decide not to tell her. The room spins, but just a bit.

The jab is deep and rough. I scream.
That really hurt.
Things that are good for you always hurt sweetheart.

I feel heat rising into my hair follicles.
Suddenly, a little man is looking up at me from the side of my raised bed.
I'm your anesthesiologist, Dr. Bliss. He is very short. His tiny hands refer to his notes.
I noticed last time they put Zofran in the IV for nausea. Did that work for you?
Yes, it was lovely. Thank you.
I am in love with this tiny man who doles out drugs.

The ride to the OR feels like a carousel. Round and round I go. My eyes spin kaleidoscopes.
And then the bliss. Only soft colors, red and green and blue.

It's over.

You did great, Marion.
Oh, thank you so much Dr. K.
How did you do?

When Your 85

The sagging old mansion of dreams
remain, as I wipe the vapor from my glasses
It's hard to see the road when
you look through kaleidoscope eyes

When you're 85 colors spin
Snow swirls round street lamps a blur
Who will live and who will die this year?
My Kaleidoscope eyes can only wonder

I see the world with kaleidoscope eyes, spinning, dizzily
churning, heading toward the end, hard to keep up
Yet...
I'm on a Carousel, trying to grab the ring, pushing on
hoping to win the prize

I am a time machine, glorifying vignettes of the past

The Wig Shop

Good morning, Marion.
Welcome to La Wig! I'm so happy to see that you are right on time for our appointment. My name is Guinevere. Let me assure you I will make this consultation as fruitful and painless as possible.

She speaks with a haughty air.

Well, thank you Guinevere. I must tell you I am feeling quite nervous and apprehensive about our meeting. I'm here because I'm so worried about my thinning hair. I hope you can help me find a solution.

I know making the decision to come here was difficult. But I promise you that your examination, diagnosis and treatment today will be beneficial. You know this is all strictly confidential.

Diagnosis? Treatment?

This tall pencil-woman of a certain age is dressed in a long black slip of a dress. Her stomach is flat and the breasts that peek out of the low-cut bodice are obviously enhanced. Her face is heavily made up with extra blush. The thick detachable eyelashes make her blink. Her hair is a cascade of long, lush, silky blond curls. It swishes left and right when she walks. It's a wig, right? Who is she kidding?

She leads me to a cavernous room, filled on three walls with rows of mannequin heads, all wearing wigs. They are an array of color, texture, and volume. Each mannequin has a face with eyes that stare out at me with lifelike expression. Some have grotesque grins, some wear subtle and sultry smiles, some have a come-hither look, and some look as anxious as I feel.

41

Marion, I want you to relax and take your time examining all of my girls. They are waiting patiently for you to choose at least one of them. They want so much to please you. I know at the end of the day you will be satisfied. I will leave you alone for a few minutes and when I return, we can start the fittings.

I think of the eyes these mannequins follow me with as I slowly pass them by. Am I crazy? I do a double take, but they are still as stone. I feel dizzy and nauseated and a bit frightened.

Every wig has a nametag; Melanie, Cassandra, Dixie, Portia, Genevieve, Traci, Brunhilda, Theresa. I see Wendy, Margaret and then Jezebel with her luscious blond head of curls. Do I detect a whiff of Jasmine as I stop to touch her? Do I feel her quiver? Medusa grins under her full head of wild stand-up writhing dreadlocks. Did Dixie just wink at me?
Oh God, where is the bathroom?

Before I can look for an escape route, I hear the click click of high-heeled shoes. Guinevere is back.
Marion, have you enjoyed your tour? I know my girls love you! Darling come with me for your fitting.

Before I can answer, Guinevere leads me to an alcove off to the left. She sits me down in a large leather beauty salon chair, adjusts the height and hovers above me holding what looks like a small nylon stocking. Without warning and with great force she presses the tight-fitting stocking onto my head. I am trapped.

Marion, I think you will like Dixie! Hold still, here she comes. She's the pixie hair style, perfect for you. She comes in many colors, even green and pink. I have tried to match your blond, gray, pathetic hair.

Pathetic? Did she say pathetic?

Guinevere is pressing Dixie down hard onto my head. I look into the mirror to see what looks like a cloche hat. It hurts and I hate it.

Perhaps better for you is my darling Brunhilde. This is a stick straight, blond Aryan wig with bangs.

Notice how beautifully she stays in motion.
I can feel the synthetic hairs swishing on my face. I look into the mirror and can only see my nose and mouth.

Don't you think it's a bit too hairy for me?
You are very hard to please, my dear. Here comes my favorite, perfect for you. Her name is Portia, melancholy like you.

Guinevere holds a long gray straggly monstrosity. She wiggles it onto my head. I look into the mirror to see an old decrepit witch. By now I have a pounding headache, I am sweating profusely, and my bowels are loosening.

Guinevere, these are all so lovely. I'm so sorry, but I need to use a restroom. It's an emergency.
Marion, you are so exasperating. The restroom is at the front of the shop. I will wait for you here.

I tear Portia from my head and race to the front of the shop. I make a last-minute vital determination. I think I can run to my car and make it home safely to my own bathroom. If I stay, I know Guinevere will come looking for me.

I am in the parking lot, a cool breeze is rustling and tossing my own lovely short hair.

On Dying

The Funeral

Marion don't turn around. You know who is heading this way.
  Oh no, you mean Aunt Dora? Marcia, why are we laughing?
I don't know. I can't help it!
  Grab Johnny and Barbara. They're too little to understand
what's gonna happen.
  Uh oh, I can feel her hot breath on my neck!

I am ten years old attending the funeral of our philandering
Grandpa Hymie.

My cousin Marcia, born six days after me, older cousin Philly
and their respective younger siblings Johnny and Barbara are all
here too. It is our first funeral.

We have been coached by our parents about this non-
traditional ritual and now we are in line to view the body.
(Traditionally Jews use a closed casket.)

It comes as a shock to see the remains of a vibrant seventy-
seven-year-old man who is no longer breathing or moving. His
face is pale, with a waxy, yellowish hew. The dabs of red color
rubbed onto the cheeks and lips, give the corpse a ghoulish
pallor. I will not forget this ever!

What has become of the handsome, flamboyant, fun-loving
grandpa who always pushed a two-dollar bill into my palm on
his rare visits?

We are told that he died on Brighton Beach after a long swim
in the ocean. A quick stroke took him the way he wanted to go.
He was alone. All that was left in the sand was a towel, his
wallet, and his watch.

What should we do? Are you going to touch him? We are
whispering.
  Are you kidding? I'm not going to touch him.
Look at his hands! They look like "House of Wax" hands.

The cousins, all in a row, are in front of the casket. We begin
to giggle. It is hard to control this reaction to our fear and
horror. We try to choke back laughter.

Older cousin Philly gets a whack on the head from Uncle Abe. My mother comes up behind me and says, *Keep moving, you've seen enough.* Aunt Fae takes little cousin John by the hand and pulls him away.

Hymie's wife, Sarah, who is still alive, looks on from the first pew. She is dressed in a long black crepe dress, eyes cast down. She has no tears for this man who caused her nothing but pain.

Here she comes. Get ready!

Ahh, Aiy, Oy, there you are, you beautiful children. Come here and give me a hug.
We turn and see the unnaturally large breasts first. The discretely lined, black lace bodice fully exposes their shape. We feel the smothering hugs and get a whiff of the damp underarms before we can see the face. She is screaming above the quiet murmur in the room.
It's aunt Dora!

Aach, *Oy, Oy, my poor shvester (sister) had to live with that terrible man. No, no, I don't speak bad of the dead. There was some good in him too. Oy, Oy, Vey. He dies on the beach like a bum. What did he have? He had nothing! The SOB had a pretty good life though. You kids don't need to hear what I tell you.*

We finally look up to see her face. Beneath the beautiful curly gray hair, we see the bright, sly blue eyes and ruddy complexion. There's a trace of sweaty fuzz, a mustache above ruby red lipstick. Then it starts.

Pooh, Pooh, Pooh on you! Kenahora, Kenahora. You are such beautiful kids; you should be well. Pooh, Pooh, Pooh! (always three times) She holds two fingers in front of her mouth. *Pooh! Pooh!*

I can feel the spray from her pursed lips.
In Jewish superstition this pooh poohing is to ward off the evil eye. Giving compliments can conjure up the devil, so you have to spit three times to keep the evil away.

Kenahora means "halt to the evil eye." We kids are doubled over with hysterical, tearful laughter.

Don't cry kids. It's okay, he was a good grandpa to you. Pooh, Pooh, Pooh, you should live and be well. Oy such beautiful children.

Thank you, Aunt Dora!

We race to the bathroom to recover.

Linda's Poem

It's February. Cold. Colder than normal for this time of year.
   A bitter wind whips off the water and cuts right through us
as my daughter and I hurry to meet a friend at work
in one of the glassed and marbled Wall Street Buildings,
when a sign on a building pique my curiosity.
   I stop to take a picture and Leah reminds me,
   This is no time for sightseeing.
   It's below zero with the wind chill factor.

Suddenly, my eye takes in a figure.
   A man sits on the sidewalk in front of a building.
I hesitate just for a second, consider the morality of what I am
about to do.
   Sans gloves in the few seconds it takes to snap the shutter,
I fear frostbite.

Afterwards, I approach him sitting there with his worldly
possessions in a brown bag beside him, sewing his coat.
   He has a look of nobility.
A dropout from the Harvard School of Divinity
I imagine, but don't ask.

In a few days tourists will come to see and celebrate,
where George Washington was inaugurated our first
President.
   I wonder what they will think of this site/sight
We don't return
   Leah is right.
It's too cold to sightsee

George Washington never slept here.

By Linda Rose

48

Roxanne and Ryan

"Ryan! Ryaaan! Where are you? Bring me the box of tissues!" Roxanne is lying in bed with an ice pack on her head. Her shoe polish black hair is sticking up in short spikes. Her nose is red and runny like a dripping faucet. "Ryan, where the hell are you? Bring me the damn tissues".

"Yeah, yeah, Roxanne, don't get your bowels in an uproar. It's your own frikin fault that you did those lines last night. I'll be there as soon as I walk the dogs. They made a mess again here in the kitchen." Ryan is shaking his moppy dirty blond head back and forth in resignation.

There was a time when Roxanne had a full-time job as a nurse and got as far as a supervisor for a decent New Jersey hospital. When she got busted for stealing too many painkillers, she not only got fired but lost her license. Ryan had been the lead acoustics technician for several rock bands in the area but now was unemployed. Roxanne and Ryan are both on disability insurance.

The day in November is dark, and the wind is blowing what's left of autumn's bright yolk-colored yellow leaves. It is the spinning touch of color that makes Roxanne smile as she looks out the window. "I've got to stop this shit. I need to get it together. Maybe if I win at poker tonight, it'll be just enough to fly down to Florida," she whispers.

"Ryan, bring me the damn tissues!"

Ryan is slamming out of the house and is running along the cracked pavement with dogs in tow. He lights a cigarette as he goes. He pulls what's left of his leather jacket close. "I've got to get out of here. Maybe I can get a gig with Charlie's band just through the holidays". His cheeks are cherry red and his breath is coming in quick gasps. The searing pain has come back in his chest. He slows his pace.

49

"Here's your damn box of tissues, Roxy." He enters the bedroom. "Time to get up and do some dishes. There's a big pool of burnt orange grease in the sink. You might also try running a vacuum cleaner over all the curly dog hair."

"FU, Ryan."
"FU, Roxanne."

Laughter. Roxanne and Ryan laugh at their own pathetic lives. They at least have each other.
"Ryan let's just smoke a joint and figure out what to do. Yeah?"

"Yeah, Roxanne."

Roxanne and Ryan 'Til Death

I'm dying Ryan, this is it
My bones are dry winter twigs
My breaths are short, cold bursts of wind
My wounds glow blood red

No Roxanne, you must stay
We have memories, laughter, show time
We are rolling stones; we keep going
It will be Vegas in the spring, they wait for us to come

Don't go Roxanne, I love you

I'm dying Ryan, this is it
No more stand-up, no more poker, no jokes
I want to sleep free of pain. Time for my Oxy?
And maybe a cigarette?

Goodbye to Bowie, my love

Your skin is pale snow
Your cheeks are fever red
Your eyes shine bright
 I see this is it

Thanks for the ride Roxanne

Thanks for the ride Ryan

Hair Today, Gone Tomorrow

Dad is funny, in a depressed sort of way

Running his fingers over his bald head
As if there was hair
Tossing his head back as if there was hair
Hair today, gone tomorrow, he would say

Riding on his shoulders at the Bronx Zoo
Hugging his dome close to my heart
Feeling his warmth
Hair today, Gone tomorrow

Fifth birthday party, dad makes a standing microphone
everyone sings into it
A lightly starched collar, silky tie
face and teeth scrubbed clean
Smelling sweet
I press my cheek to his

Running behind me on my first two-wheeler ride
He barely touches the seat
We fly around the bike path to circle the play ground
He lets go and I am free

At my wedding, dad, perfectly groomed
trembling, walks me down the aisle
His blue eyes watery
as he gives me away
Hair today, Gone tomorrow

Cancer
Dad is very quiet
At home his shallow breathing watches the game
On a morphine high

Dad wants a dinner alone with me in a restaurant

We sit across from each other with wistful smiles
Marion, I never told you
Frozen, I pause and wait, pause and wait
I love you so much, was too shy to say.
But I'm dying now
No, not yet, dad
Hair today, gone tomorrow

The taxi is called
Dad insists on going to the hospital alone
He turns and waves to us
He never comes home

Author Bio

Marion owes her love for reading and writing to her mother, Lena Paula. From earliest childhood, her mom read stories to her every day and encouraged her to write her own.

It came together twelve years ago at the Lawrence Library Writers Group. There, with excellent feedback, she honed her skills and shared her stories and poetry.

Marion's work has been published several times in *Back in the Bronx* and *Kelsey Review*.

Her book *Grandma, Tell Us a Story, Tales of a daring hypochondriac* can be found on Amazon.

Pollack's education background includes a BS degree from Cortland College, master's Degrees from Northeastern University and The College of NJ.

Marion has been a teacher, college and guidance counselor, and substance abuse counselor at Hightstown High School. She continued her career as a therapist at Alexander Road Associates and Aroga Behavioral Health in Princeton, NJ.

She and her husband Bob live in Lawrenceville, NJ. They have two grown children and six grandchildren.

Marion and Bob at Grounds for Sculpture